This edition published by Parragon Inc. 2013

Parragon Inc.
440 Park Avenue South, 13th Floor
New York, NY 10016
www.parragon.com

Edited by Gemma Louise Lowe
Designed by Pete Hampshire
Production by Charlene Vaughan

ISBN 978-1-4723-2016-2

Printed in China

Mickey
and the
Beanstalk

PaRRagon

Bath · New York · Singapore · Hong Kong · Cologne · Delhi
Melbourne · Amsterdam · Johannesburg · Shenzhen

Long, long ago, there was a place where it was sunny every day. It was called Happy Valley. Everything there was pretty and green and … happy.

High on a hilltop overlooking the valley stood a castle. Inside were many beautiful things, but the most beautiful thing of all was a golden harp.

This was no ordinary harp, though. This harp sang sweetly and had the face of an angel. Its magical music cast a spell of peace over Happy Valley.

One day, a mysterious shadow darkened the valley. When it went away, the harp had disappeared! Without the harp, the magic spell was broken. Soon, the people grew sad and hungry.

Three farmers were sadder and hungrier than anyone else— Farmer Mickey, Farmer Donald, and Farmer Goofy. They only had a slice of bread, and a few beans between them.

They decided that the only thing they could do to survive was to trade their cow for food.

So, Farmer Mickey went to sell the cow. On his way to the
market, Mickey met an old man.

"Hello, Farmer Mickey," said the man. "Where are you going?"

"I'm headed to the market to sell my cow," Mickey explained.

The old man looked at the cow. "I'll give you these magical
beans for her. If you plant them under a full moon, they will
grow right up to the sky!"

Farmer Mickey was curious, and there was a full moon that
night, so he agreed to trade his cow for the beans.

When Mickey returned home, he showed Donald and Goofy the beans.

"Three beans!" his friends cried angrily when Mickey held out his hand. "We can't live on three beans!"

"These are magic beans," Mickey tried to explain, but his friends wouldn't listen. Donald grabbed the beans, and threw them on the ground. They bounced once, twice, and then landed in a hole in the floor.

The three farmers crawled into bed hungrier than ever. They didn't know what they would do.

Then, under the bright moonlight, something strange happened. The beans began to grow. A stem formed, and quickly turned into a huge stalk.

The beanstalk climbed all the way into the sky, carrying the farmhouse with it!

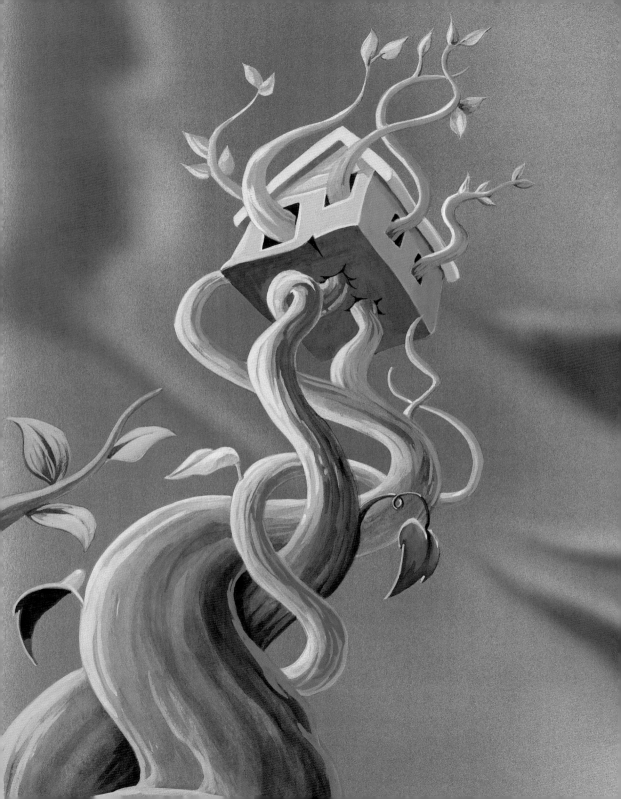

When the hungry farmers awoke the next morning, they
looked out the window … Happy Valley was gone! They
were in a strange land on top of the clouds.

Mickey pointed to a giant castle in the distance.

"Whoever lives there must have plenty of food. Maybe
he'll share."

The three friends ran to the castle. They helped each
other climb the stairs, and then slid under the door.

When they finally got inside, the three farmers spotted huge bowls and plates filled with food. They had never seen so much to eat in one place!

The farmers ran to the table and started eating everything in sight.

Soon the farmers were too full to eat
another bite. Suddenly, they heard
a tiny voice call out to them
from a chest on the table.

"Who are you?"
Mickey asked.

"It is I, the golden
harp," said the tiny
voice. "A wicked giant
stole me, and brought
me here to sing for
him. The sound helps
him sleep."

The farmers were
frightened when they
heard the word "giant."

Just then, everything in the room started to shake. Heavy footsteps thundered toward them.

A voice roared out, "Fee-fi-fo-fum! I smell ... a pot roast!"

Mickey, Donald and Goofy hid behind a sugar bowl. The Giant entered the room. He was taller than ten men, and looked stronger than forty!

The Giant started to make himself a big meal.

As he reached for the sugar, the three friends scurried to find new hiding places. Mickey hid in the bread, but the Giant used the bread to make a sandwich and Mickey got stuck inside! The Giant was about to take a bite when he noticed the farmer wriggling around.

"Gotcha!" the Giant cried, grabbing Mickey.

Then, he spotted Donald and Goofy as they tried to run away. They weren't quick enough and the Giant caught them and stuffed them into his giant hand along with Mickey.

The Giant dropped
all of them into the
chest where he was
keeping the harp.
Luckily, Mickey was
able to escape.

The Giant grabbed the harp
before he locked the chest and
slipped the key into his pocket.
He hadn't noticed that Mickey
was free.

The Giant sat down on a nearby chair, and placed the harp on the table in front of him. The harp sang sweetly and soon lulled him to sleep. When Mickey heard the Giant snoring, he climbed down a piece of thread.

Then, ever so
carefully, he climbed
into the Giant's pocket,
and took the key. The
Giant's pocket was
very dusty and it made
Mickey sneeze!

The Giant stirred in his sleep.
So, Mickey grabbed the key
and climbed back up the thread
as quickly as he could. He let
his friends out of the box, and
grabbed the harp. The sleepy
Giant checked his pocket—the
key was missing! He looked
around the room and saw Mickey,
Goofy and Donald creeping
toward the door.

"Come back here!" he roared.

Goofy and Donald ran away with the harp. Mickey knew he had to distract the Giant.

"You can't catch me!" he yelled. The angry Giant ran toward Mickey, who jumped onto a bottle of carbonated water. He popped the cork and flew right out the window.

"Over here!" Mickey said, but the Giant was not fast enough to catch him.

"So long!" he cried as he jumped off the cork, and chased after his friends. The Giant thundered after him, shouting for the farmers to bring back his harp.

The ground shook with every step the Giant took, but the farmers kept going. They climbed down the beanstalk as fast as they could. Donald, and Goofy reached the ground first.

While Mickey hurried the rest of the way, his friends grabbed a saw and began to cut down the stem.

The Giant had followed them, and was climbing down, down, down. Donald and Goofy kept sawing, as quickly as they could.

Suddenly, the beanstalk
began to wobble, until
finally, it toppled over.
The Giant crashed to the
ground and was silent.

With the Giant gone, the farmers took the
golden harp back to the castle on the hilltop.

Happy Valley was a very cheerful place once more. And no one was more pleased than the three brave friends—Farmer Mickey, Farmer Donald, and Farmer Goofy. They had saved the harp and Happy Valley!

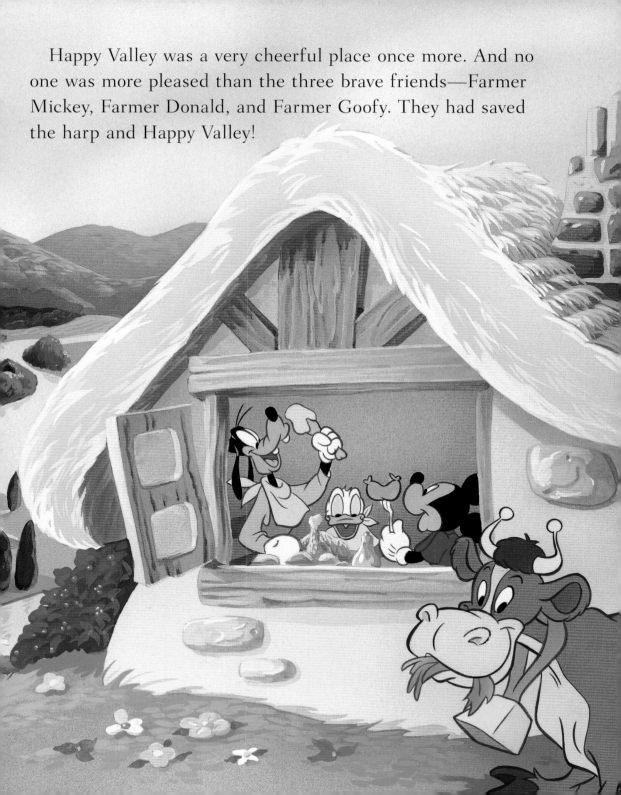